Baby Bird's First Nest

FRANK ASCH

SCHOLASTIC INC.

New York Toronto London Auckland Sydney
Mexico City New Delhi Hong Kong

ISBN0-439-16574-1

12 11 10 9 8 7 6 5 4 3 2 1   0 1 2 3 4 5/0

Printed in the U.S.A.   09

First Scholastic printing, March 2000

The illustrations in this book were drawn in pen and ink, and colorized by Devin Asch in Adobe Photoshop.
The display type was set in Elroy.
The text type.was set in Goudy Catalogue.
Designed by Lydia D'moch

To Devin

One night Baby Bird rolled over in her sleep, tumbled out
of her nest, and woke up with a thump.

Baby Bird wasn't hurt, but she was very frightened. Darkness loomed all around her. Even the moon looked cold and scary.

"Mama, help me!" she cried.

But Mama Bird was fast asleep.

Beneath Baby Bird's tree lived Little Frog.
"What are you croaking about?" he asked.

"I fell out of my nest," Baby Bird said, flapping her tiny wings, "and I can't get back."

Little Frog climbed out of his pond. "I was going for a moonlight swim. Do you want to come along?"

"I just want to go back to my mama and my nest!" sniffled Baby Bird.

"Don't worry, your mama will find you in the morning," said Little Frog.

"The morning's a long way off," replied Baby Bird. "What shall I do till then?"

"Why not build your own nest?" asked Little Frog.

"I've never built a nest before," sighed Baby Bird.

"Neither have I," said Little Frog. "But I'd be glad to help you."

So Baby Bird and Little Frog set to work building a
nest. They gathered twigs and pine needles to make the

outside. Then they lined the inside with birch bark and
deer grass.

When the nest was finished, Baby Bird hopped inside
and chirped, "It's beautiful! And cozy, too!"

With a skip and a jump, Little Frog flipped himself into
the nest. "Kind of scratchy for my taste," he croaked.

"Of course you'd think that. You're a frog," said Baby
Bird. "But it's perfect for me." Then she sighed with relief.
"My very first nest."

Baby Bird snuggled down and soon began to feel sleepy.
But Little Frog sat up straight.
  "I hear paws," he croaked.

"Quick, follow me!"
Little Frog leaped out of the nest and into the pond.
Kerplunk!

Baby Bird looked up and saw a hungry raccoon. *If I jump in the pond, I'll drown,* she thought. So she scrambled out of her nest and fled in the opposite direction.

Baby Bird spied a low branch above her head. She crouched down, flapped her tiny wings, and hopped up onto the branch.

Raccoon stood on his hind legs.

Baby Bird closed her eyes, trembling with fear.

But Raccoon couldn't reach her.

Raccoon hunted in the water until he found a fish to eat. When he was gone, Little Frog swam ashore and went looking for Baby Bird. He looked in the nest. It was empty. He looked behind the nest and even under the nest.

"Oh my," he croaked. "Raccoon got Baby Bird!"

"No, he didn't. I'm up here."
"How did you get up there?" asked Little Frog.
"I hopped up," replied Baby Bird.

"If you can hop up there, you can hop back to your nest," said Little Frog.

"I can't hop that far!" gasped Baby Bird.

"Sure you can," said Little Frog, "if you take it one
hop at a time. Here, I'll show you." And he hopped to
Baby Bird's perch.

"Now follow me," he said, and hopped to a branch
above her head. "Can you do that?"

"Sure," chirped Baby Bird.

"Good," said Little Frog, and he hopped to the next
higher branch.

Little Frog hopped, and Baby Bird followed higher and higher, all the way back to her nest.

"Mama, I'm home," she cried.

Slowly Mama Bird opened her eyes. "Of course you are, my darling," she said with a yawn. "But what are you doing out there?"

Mama Bird lifted Baby Bird into the nest.

"Mama," cried Baby Bird, "I've had the most wonderful adventure!"

"Yes, yes." Mama Bird yawned again. "You can tell me all about it in the morning."

Soon Mama Bird was fast asleep.

"Your mama's nice," said Little Frog.

"Do you want to sleep in our nest tonight?" asked Baby Bird.

Little Frog thought for a moment. "Too scratchy," he replied.

"So what are you going to do now?" asked Baby Bird.

"I guess I'll finish that moonlight swim," said Little Frog. "Get ready for the highest dive you ever saw!"

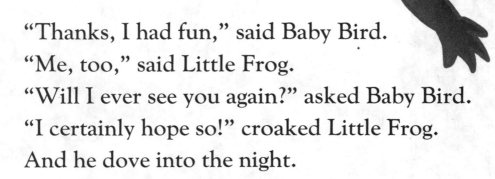

"Thanks, I had fun," said Baby Bird.

"Me, too," said Little Frog.

"Will I ever see you again?" asked Baby Bird.

"I certainly hope so!" croaked Little Frog.

And he dove into the night.